WHERE HAVE YOU BEEN?

Where Have You Been?

by MARGARET WISE BROWN
Illustrated by BARBARA COONEY

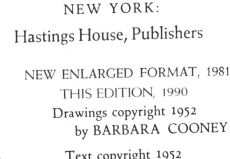

NEW YORK:

Hastings House, Publishers

NEW ENLARGED FORMAT, 1981
THIS EDITION, 1990

Printed in U.S.A.

Little Old Cat
Little Old Cat
Where have you been?
To see this and that
Said the Little Old Cat
That's where I've been.

Little Old Squirrel
Little Old Squirrel
Where have you been?
I've been out on a whirl
Said the Little Old Squirrel
That's where I've been.

Little Old Fish
Little Old Fish
Where do you swim?
Wherever I wish
Said the Little Old Fish
That's where I swim.

Little Brown Bird
Little Brown Bird
Where do you fly?
I fly in the sky
Said the Little Brown Bird
That's where I fly.

Little Old Horse
Little Old Horse
Where have you been?
In the clover, of course
Said the Little Old Horse
That's where I've been.

Little Old Toad
Little Old Toad
Where have you been?
I've been way up the road
Said the Little Old Toad
That's where I've been.

Little Old Frog
Little Old Frog
Where have you been?
I've been sitting on a log
Said the Little Old Frog
That's where I've been.

Little Old Mole
Little Old Mole
Where have you been?
Down a long dark hole
Said the Little Old Mole
That's where I've been.

Little Old Bee
Little Old Bee
Where have you been?
In a pink apple tree
Said the Little Old Bee
That's where I've been.

Little Old Whale
Little Old Whale
Where do you sail?
Down under the gale
Said the Little Old Whale
That's where I sail.

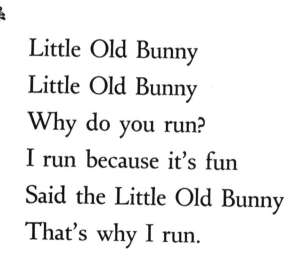

Little Old Bunny
Little Old Bunny
Why do you run?
I run because it's fun
Said the Little Old Bunny
That's why I run.

Little Old Lion
Little Old Lion
Where have you been?
Where the jungle grows dim
Said the Little Old Lion
That's where I've been.

Little Old Mouse
Little Old Mouse
Why run down the clock?
To see if the tick
Comes after the tock
I run down the clock.

Little Old Rook
Little Old Rook
Where do you look?
At the very last page
Of this very same book
Said the Little Old Rook.